12-03-02

12-03-02

THE POLAR BEARS ARE HUNGRY

BY CAROL CARRICK

ILLUSTRATED BY PAUL CARRICK

Clarion Books / New York

Clarion Books
a Houghton Mifflin Company imprint
215 Park Avenue South, New York, NY 10003
Text copyright © 2002 by Carol Carrick
Illustrations copyright © 2002 by Paul Carrick

The illustrations were executed in acrylic paint.
The text was set in 18-point Seagull.

For information about permission to reproduce selections from this book, write to Permissions,
Houghton Mifflin Company, 215 Park Avenue South, New York, NY 10003.

www.houghtonmifflinbooks.com

Manufactured in China.

Library of Congress Cataloging-in-Publication Data

Carrick, Carol.
The polar bears are hungry / by Carol Carrick ; illustrated by Paul Carrick.
p.   cm.
Summary: A mother polar bear takes care of her new cubs, but as temperatures rise, she finds
it increasingly difficult to get enough to eat.
ISBN 0-618-15962-2
1. Polar bear—Juvenile fiction 2. Polar bear—Fiction. 3. Bears—Fiction. I. Carrick, Paul, ill. II. Title.
PZ10.3.C245 Po 2002   [E]—dc21   2002005912

SCP   10 9 8 7 6 5 4 3 2 1

To Norton and, especially, Trixie, who was a fine polar bear mother.

Many thanks to Ron Martini, Keeper of North American Mammals,
Roger Williams Park Zoo, Providence, Rhode Island, as well as the staffs
of Churchill Northern Studies Center and Wapusk National Park, Manitoba,
for their help with this book.
—C.C. & P.C.

It is dark in Arctic winter.
The sea is covered with ice.

On the land, inside a snowbank,
two polar bear cubs are born.
For months their drowsy mother rocks them.
Warms them with her breath.
Feeds them while they grow strong.

The cubs stumble out of their cozy den
for the first time.
They squint in the light.
Roll down the snowbank.
Tumble.

Soon the bears move toward the sea.
Mother Bear is hungry.
She hasn't eaten for months.
Her body needs food
so she will have milk for her cubs.

Mother sniffs the air.
She can smell seal from a long way off.
Seal fat is her favorite food.
The fat layer under their skin
keeps seals and bears warm.

Patiently, she waits by a hole in the ice
where seals come up to breathe.
She waits.
And waits.

A seal rises.
Quickly,
Mother hauls it up.
The cubs get their first taste of seal.
They like it, too.

Spring is coming.
Each day the sun is warmer.
The bear cubs slip and slide on the ice.
Chase each other.
Bite.
Splash in puddles.

The ice pack is breaking up.
The bears ride the ice floes, hunting for seals.

The seals are sunning themselves.
Mother shows the cubs how to catch one.
She flattens herself like a rug.
The cubs watch as she wriggles across the ice,
pushing with her toes.
C-l-o-s-e-r, c-l-o-s-e-r.
She makes a dash—
she pounces!

With an explosion of barks,
the seals scatter.
Mother snatches one.

The ice floes shrink even smaller.
Mother swims with the cubs on her back.
Soon they paddle on their own
with wide, webbed front paws.

The bears must fatten up before the ice melts.
Mother sees an ice floe loaded with seals,
shoving each other to get more space.
She glides toward them,
only her face showing.

With a mighty heave,
she is on the ice.
Panic!
The seals dive in all directions.
They swim too fast for Mother to catch one.

Now the ice is gone.
For months it is warm—
too warm for bears.
Flies buzz in their ears.
Blur their eyes.
Get up their noses.

Sometimes they eat a little grass
and some berries,
a dead seal,
or a bird that washes up on shore.
This is a hungry time for bears.

When the days grow colder,
the bears move north,
where ice will be forming.
Passing a village,
they pick through its garbage dump for food.
People make loud noises
and frighten them off.

But the bears return,
bold because they are hungry
and Mother needs milk for her cubs.
This time they come into the village,
where they smell food.

Children on their way to school
see the bears breaking into a house.
Wildlife officers come
to drug Mother and her cubs
so they can safely move them
to a special jail for bears.

As soon as Mother Bear can stand,
she tries to escape from the cell.
But the walls are thick and the bars are strong.
She paces.
Moans.
Still, Mother is relieved
that the cubs are with her
so she can protect them
from the strange sounds and smells.

Wind shrieks through the long, cold night.
Ice cracks and groans
while the sea freezes over.
Now the bears can be set loose.

Free again,
the bears have one
overpowering need.
They set off at a trot,
following
the scent
of seal.

That night the snow drifts against Mother's back.
The cubs snuggle into the curve of her body.
Her milk is rich.
Their stomachs are full.
And tomorrow will bring more good hunting.

AUTHOR'S NOTE

During October and November, the pregnant polar bears of the Arctic dig a den in the snow and doze. By late December, one to three cubs the size of guinea pigs are born. The mother stays in the den and her cubs nurse and sleep until spring. By then, she has been fasting for eight months. When the mother and her cubs emerge, the cubs weigh about twenty pounds. For the first two and a half years of their lives, they stay close to her, nursing and learning to hunt.

Seal fat, especially fat from baby seals, is the polar bear's primary food. A polar bear's long head and neck enable it to reach deep into a seal's den or into its air hole in the ice and pull up a two-hundred-pound seal. Although the bears are excellent swimmers, they do not swim fast enough to catch seals in the water. Bears need ice to hunt seals, so they spend the summer months in a state of walking hibernation, living on the fat stored under their skin.

Global warming has shortened the time during which polar bears can successfully hunt seals. In recent years, when the ice has melted early, some hungry animals have learned to scavenge in areas where people live. Those captured are given water but no food in the hope of discouraging them from returning. Since a mother with cubs is under great stress to survive, she and her cubs are freed as quickly as possible.

A short hunting season can leave a mother in a weakened condition. Her milk will not be nutritious, and her cubs will have a poor chance of survival. In this way, global warming, as well as mining, offshore drilling, and the pollution of the food chain, is changing the once remote and pristine world of the polar bear.